Highlights Puzzle Readers

LEVEL 2

LET'S READ, READ, READ

FLY THE SKIES

By Michelle Portice
Art by Mitch Mortimer

HIGHLIGHTS PRESS
Honesdale, Pennsylvania

Stories + Puzzles = Reading Success!

Dear Parents,

Highlights Puzzle Readers are an innovative approach to learning to read that combines puzzles and stories to build motivated, confident readers.

Developed in collaboration with reading experts, the stories and puzzles are seamlessly integrated so that readers are encouraged to read the story, solve the puzzles, and then read the story again. This helps increase vocabulary and reading fluency and creates a satisfying reading experience for any kind of learner. In addition, solving Hidden Pictures puzzles fosters important reading and learning skills such as:

- shape and letter recognition
- sound-letter relationships
- visual discrimination
- logic
- flexible thinking
- sequencing

With high-interest stories, humorous characters, and trademark puzzles, Highlights Puzzle Readers offer a winning combination for inspiring young learners to love reading.

This is Kit.

This is Kaboodle.

They love to travel. You can help them on each adventure.

As you read the story, find the objects in each Hidden Pictures puzzle.

Then check the Packing List on pages 30–31 to make sure you found everything.

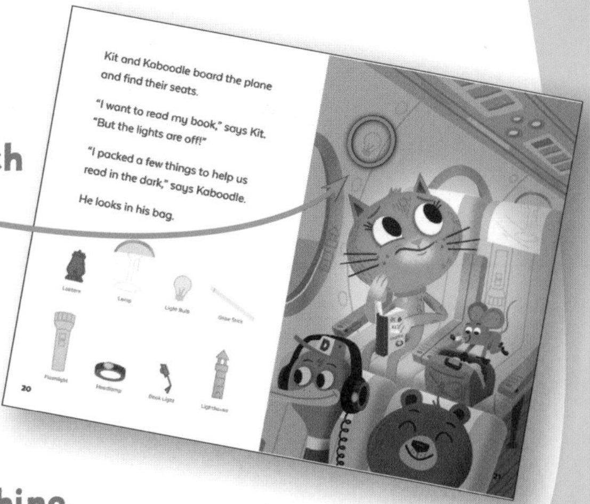

Happy reading!

This winter is very cold and snowy.
Kit and Kaboodle want to go to a warm place.

“We can go to Sun Island,” says Kit.

“That sounds fun!” says Kaboodle.

“Let’s look at the map,” says Kit.
“No roads go there.
No boats go there.
No trains go there.”

“How will we get there?” asks Kaboodle.

"We can fly on a plane!" says Kaboodle.

"I've never been on a plane before," says Kit.

"Me neither," says Kaboodle. "I can't wait!"

"Let's pack," says Kaboodle.

Kit finds a small suitcase.

"I hope this is not too big," she says.

Kaboodle finds a big suitcase.

"I hope this is not too small," he says.

Kit packs a few things.
“I’m ready!” she says.

Kaboodle packs a few things.
Then he packs more things.

“There is so much to pack,” he says.
“I hope I’m not packing all night!”

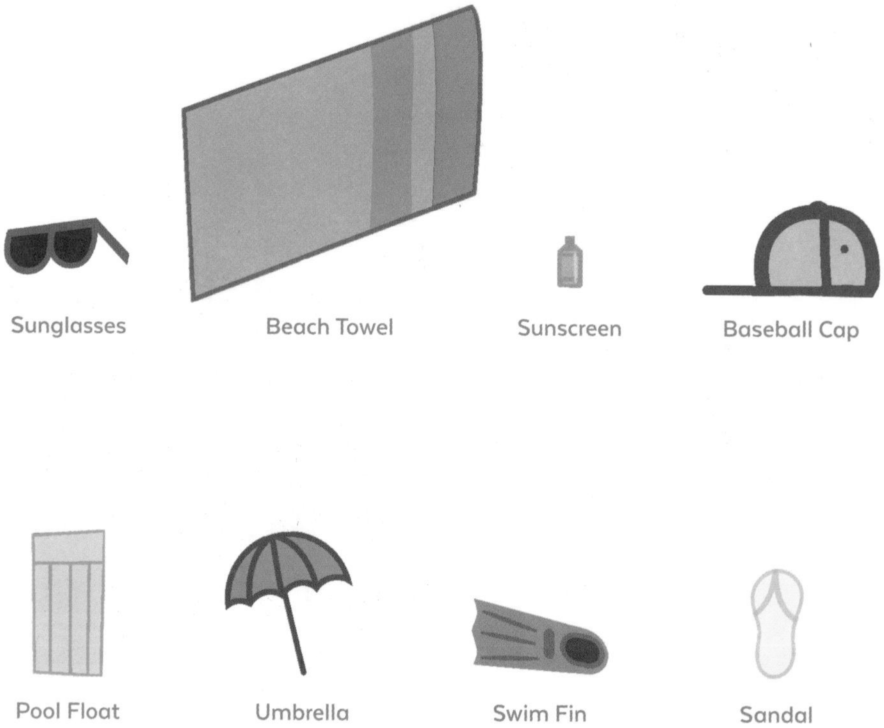

The next day, Kit and Kaboodle go to the airport.

"That plane is taking off," says Kit. "I wonder where it is going."

"That plane is landing," says Kaboodle. "I wonder where it came from."

"We'll be on our plane soon," says Kit.

"Not soon enough," says Kaboodle.

"I can't wait!"

“There’s our gate,” says Kit.

“Our flight leaves in two hours,” says Kaboodle.

“We can read while we wait,” says Kit.

“I packed some things to read,” says Kaboodle.

He looks in his suitcase.

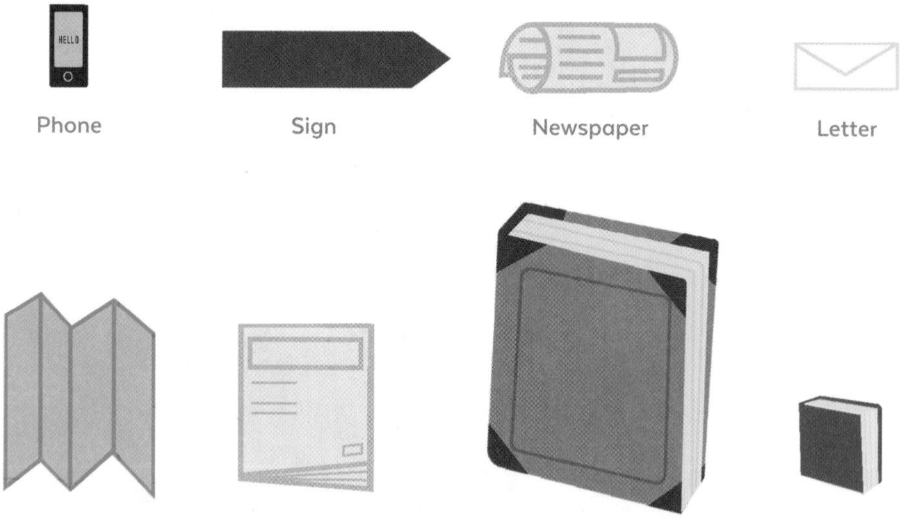

CHECK IN
HELLO
FLY

Kit and Kaboodle get their tickets. They watch their suitcases disappear.

"Our suitcases will be on our plane soon," says Kaboodle.

"Not soon enough," says Kit. "I can't wait!"

"I'm glad I don't have to carry my bag with me," says Kit.

"I'm glad I also packed a little bag to carry on the plane," says Kaboodle.

"There's our gate," says Kaboodle. "Our flight leaves in two hours."

"What can we do while we wait?" asks Kit.

"I packed a few games we can play," says Kaboodle.

He looks in his bag.

Yo-Yo

Marble

Playing Cards

Die

Top

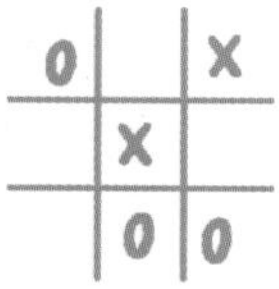
Tic-Tac-Toe

Puzzle Piece

Game Piece

SUN ISLAND
FLIGHT A73
10:30AM DEPART
2:30PM ARRIVAL
STATUS ON TIME
AIR
KIT

Kit and Kaboodle play games while they wait to board the plane.

"It's time to board!" says Kaboodle.

"Let's go!" says Kit.

"Look," says Kaboodle.

"I see a cart with five bags."

"I found it!" says Kit.

"I see a cart with four bags."

"I found it!" says Kaboodle.

Kit and Kaboodle board the plane and find their seats.

"I want to read my book," says Kit. "But the lights are off!"

"I packed a few things to help us read in the dark," says Kaboodle.

He looks in his bag.

KIT
SKETCH
D

Kit and Kaboodle buckle their seat belts.

The pilot makes an announcement.

The plane goes down the runway.

Then the plane takes off
and soars into the sky.

“We’re flying!” says Kit.

“Hooray!” says Kaboodle.

Kit and Kaboodle read,
then watch the clouds go by.

"We still have an hour before we land,"
says Kit. "Let's have a snack."

"I packed a few fruits we can eat,"
says Kaboodle.

He looks in his bag.

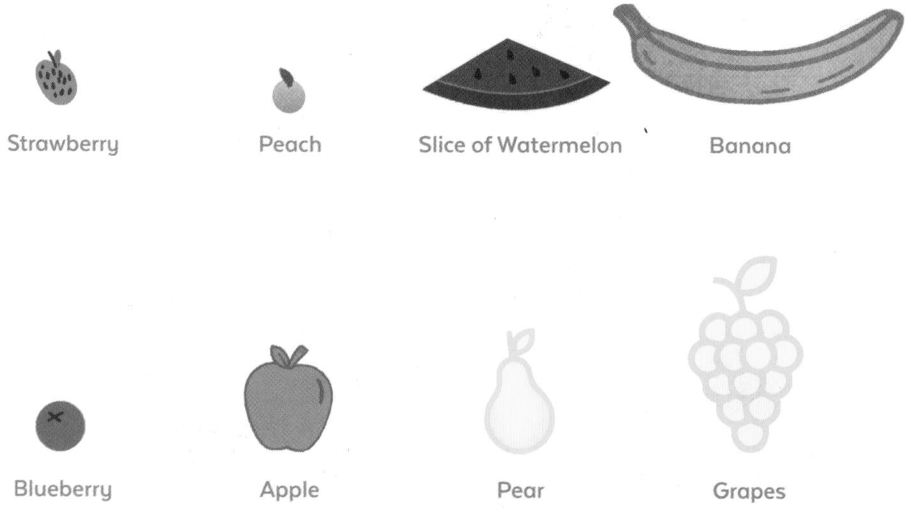

KIT
SKETCH

The plane starts to land.

"We're almost there!" says Kit.

"Look!" says Kaboodle. "I see the beach."

"Look!" says Kit. "I see palm trees."

The plane lands on the runway.
Kit and Kaboodle get off the plane.

“We’re here!” says Kit.

“Flying is so much fun,” says Kaboodle.

“We make a good team,” says Kit.

“Where should we go
on our next trip?” asks Kaboodle.

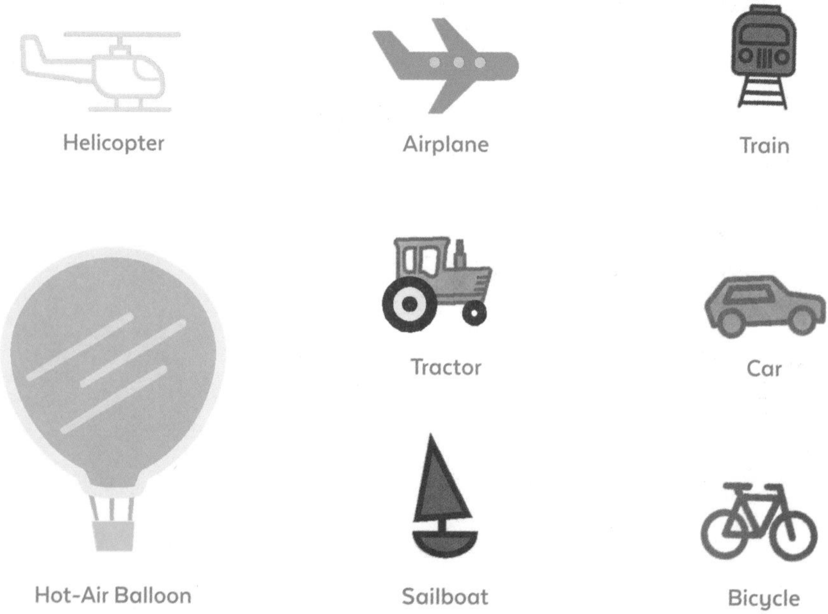

WELCOME TO
SUN ISLAND

Did you find all the things Kit an

Airplane

Apple

Banana

Baseball Cap

Book Light

Car

Dictionary

Die

Headlamp

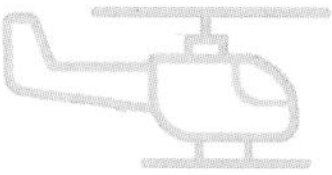
Helicopter

Hot-Air Balloon

Lamp

Magazine

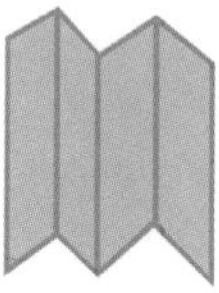
Map

Marble

Newspaper

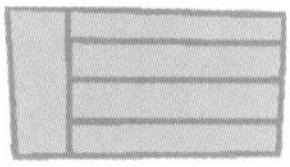
Pool Float

Puzzle Piece

Sailboat

Sandal

Sunscreen

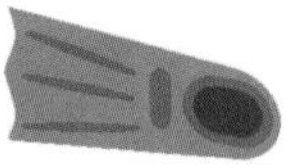
Swim Fin

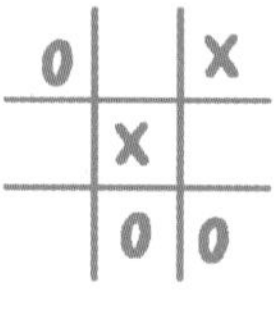

Tic-Tac-Toe

Top

aboodle packed for their trip?

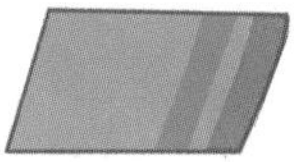
Beach Towel

Bicycle

Blueberry

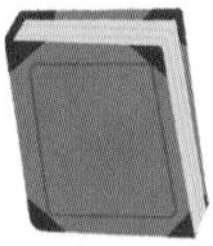
Book

Flashlight

Game Piece

Glow Stick

Grapes

Lantern

Letter

Lighthouse

Light Bulb

Peach

Pear

Phone

Playing Cards

Sign

Slice of Watermelon

Strawberry

Sunglasses

Tractor

Train

Umbrella

Yo-Yo

Published by Highlights Press
815 Church Street
Honesdale, Pennsylvania 18431
ISBN (paperback): 978-1-64472-198-8
ISBN (hardcover): 978-1-64472-199-5
ISBN (ebook): 978-1-64472-243-5

Library of Congress Control Number: 2020949584
Manufactured in Melrose Park, IL, USA
Mfg. 03/2021

First edition
Visit our website at Highlights.com.
10 9 8 7 6 5 4 3 2 1

This book has been officially leveled with both the F&P Text Level Gradient™ Leveling System and the Lexile® Text Measure.

For assistance in the preparation of this book, the editors would like to thank Vanessa Maldonado, MSEd, MS Literacy Ed. K–12, Reading/LA Consultant Cert., K–5 Literacy Instructional Coach; and Gina Shaw.